To our
Granny
with lots of
chatterings.

This edition is published and
distributed exclusively by
Discovery Toys, Inc.,
Martinez, CA

First published 1989 by Walker Books Ltd., London

© 1989 Marcia Williams

Printed in Belgium

ISBN 0-939979-39-X

WHEN I WAS LITTLE

Marcia Williams

DISCOVERY TOYS, INC.

Whenever my granny comes to stay,

she always says to me . . .

When I was little

there were fairies at the bottom of my garden

and storks left babies under gooseberry bushes.

It never rained in the summer

and every Christmas was a white Christmas.

When I was little

we walked four miles to school

and school days were the happiest of all.

When I was little

ice cream tasted of cream

and lollipops lasted all day long.

When I was little

we did not have television,

so we made our own fun and games.

There were no rockets

or men on the moon.

When I was little

we didn't have these . . .

but we did have these.

When I was little

there were no jumbo jets,

but there were steam trains.

When I was little

the dark was very frightening

and my room was full of ghosts.

When I was little

if you made an ugly face

and the wind changed,

it stuck – forever!

When I was little

bears ate you up

if you walked

on the lines

of the squares.

When I was little

girls always wore dresses

and little boys had scratched knees

because they always wore shorts.

When I was little

every beach was sandy

SUMMER

AUTUMN

WINTER

SPRING

and every holiday filled with laughter.

Babies never cried

and Daddy always knew best.

When I was little

grown-ups were very wise

and we believed everything they told us.

We ate crusts to make our hair curl

and carrots to help us see in the dark.

until I fell asleep – just like you.

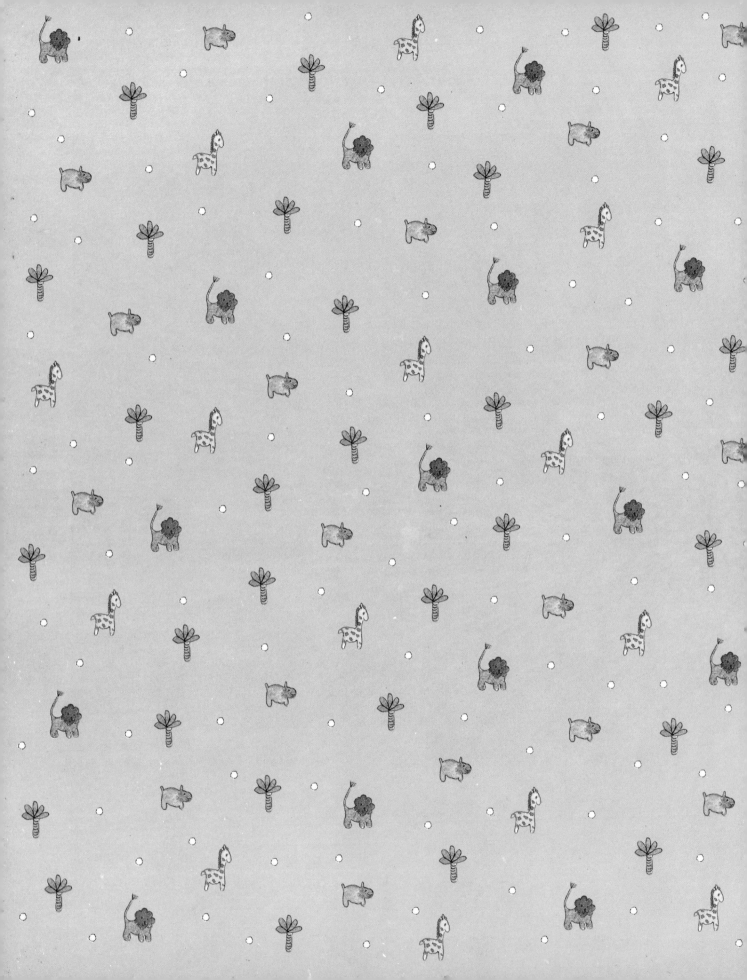